漂鳥集

Stray Birds

泰戈爾 Rabindranath Tagore 著　傅一勤 譯

國家圖書館出版品預行編目資料

漂鳥集：新譯泰戈爾詩集／泰戈爾（Rabindranath Tagore)著；傅一勤譯.修訂一版.—臺北市：
書林, 2006〔民95〕
面; 公分.
譯自：Stray Birds
ISBN 957-445- 124-0 （平裝）
867.51 94023486

書林譯詩 15

漂鳥集：新譯泰戈爾詩集

著　　者 泰戈爾（Rabindranath Tagore）
譯　　者 傅一勤
執行編輯 張麗芳
美術設計 徐子婷
出 版 者 書林出版有限公司
地　　址 100台北市羅斯福路四段60號三樓
電　　話 02-23684938・02-23687226
傳　　真 02-66329771・02-23636630
發 行 人 蘇正隆
出版經理 蘇恆隆
經銷事業 02-23684938#118・129 傳真02-66329770
學校業務 02-23687226・04-23763799・07-2290300
郵　　撥 15743873・書林出版有限公司
網　　址 http://www.bookman.com.tw
經銷代理 紅螞蟻圖書有限公司
台北市內湖區舊宗路二段121巷號四樓
電話 02-27953656（代表號） 傳真 02-27954100
印　　刷 凱立國際資訊股份有限公司
出版日期 2006年2月修訂一版，2006年12月二刷
定　　價 150元
I S B N 957-445-124-0

泰戈爾小傳

泰戈爾 (Rabindranath Tagore, 1861～1941) 于一八六一年五月六日，生於印度加爾各答 (Calcutta)，出身印度的望族。於一八七七年赴英修習法律，不旋踵放棄學業，返回印度，興趣逐漸轉入文學創作。一生創作極豐，包括約五十本戲劇，一百本詩集，四十部長短篇小說，及小品論文等多種。一九一三年獲諾貝爾文學獎，爲東方作家獲此殊榮的第一人，並由英國女王封爲爵士 (後因不滿英國對印度無理的統紿憤而退還英國政府)。其獲獎作品，主要爲《祭壇佳里》(*Gitanjali*，國內有良莠多種譯本，亦有人譯爲《頌歌集》)。當時歐洲各國推薦了總共二十八位之多相當具有分量的作家 (如英國的哈代Thomas Hardy)，參加角逐此獎。推選經過當然有一番周折，不過最後終於選中了泰戈爾。

其實，泰翁有許多著名的作品都是在這之後完成的，如本詩集《漂鳥集》 (*Stray Birds*，早年鄭振鐸曾譯爲《飛鳥集》) 便是完成於一九一六年。論者曾譽泰翁這本詩集爲雋品中之雋品，或者說是一串串現代化了的東方思想的珠玉，誠哉斯言。泰氏的另一名著《新月集》 (*The Crescent Moon*, 1913)，純粹是一本謳歌人生和大自然的散文詩集，二者皆十分受中國讀者的喜愛，對中國當時的文壇影響很大。

泰翁於一九二四年訪問中國，曾在北京大學作公開演講，由徐志摩擔任翻譯，造成極大轟動。一九三七年中日戰事爆發，曾爲文嚴厲譴責日本的侵略行爲，表現出高度的國際正義感，令人敬佩。從一九四〇年十一月起，泰戈爾的身體狀況日益惡化，一九四一年八月七日病逝於故鄉加爾各答，享年八十歲。

目　錄

Stray Birds

譯　序

印度大文豪泰戈爾，對中國讀者來說，一點也不陌生。他的重要著作，自從他得到諾貝爾文學獎 (1913) 以來，我國陸續都有譯本問世，而且同一著作常有好幾個譯本。這也難怪，據說連印度人也常說，每天讀泰戈爾一句詩，世上一切的痛苦便立刻忘了。

我國最早翻譯泰氏作品的應是鄭振鐸先生，而他首先所選譯的便是泰氏的著名短詩集*Stray Birds*，譯名作《飛鳥集》，出版於1922年，距今已七十餘年。當時我國的讀者，非常醉心於這本詩集，好像他的每一句話，都正敲中了中國人的心弦，對於我國文壇的影響至大。比如冰心女士當年名噪一時的短詩集子《繁星》和《春水》，很顯然皆受到鄭譯《飛鳥集》很深的影響，甚至因此在當時文壇上掀起了一陣小詩熱。

自此以後，每隔若干年便可以看到泰氏*Stray Birds*新的譯本問世，但以後多採用另一新的譯名《漂鳥集》(漂乃漂泊之意，據糜文開先生說，此一譯名係由他本人所創)。目前，就我所蒐羅到的便有四種譯本(實際當不止此數)，其版本出處如次：

《泰戈爾詩集》(含漂鳥集) 糜文開等譯

　　三民書局出版1963 (但序於1948年)

《失群的鳥》(即漂鳥集，英漢對照)　周策縱譯

晨鐘出版社1971（篇末註1954完成）

《泰戈爾全集》（含漂鳥集，英漢對照）尚適譯

普天出版社1972

《泰戈爾全集》（含漂鳥集，未署譯者姓名）

江南出版社1981

以上四種譯本，唯有江南版未署譯者姓名，但根據其序文 (稱爲「新序」) 曰，「我譯泰戈爾的《漂鳥集》是在一九二二年的夏天……」。由此可以推斷，此本應係鄭振鐸氏所譯無疑。至於原譯書名《飛鳥集》，據說後來再版也改了，大概就是現在這樣。序文又說，早先譯本並不完全，約只占原文的四分之三，現在所出的才是全譯本，並且說是「第一次的全譯本」。但這個本子到底是哪一年出版，江南版所載的年代自不可靠。關於本詩集的名稱，唯有周譯《失群的鳥》與眾不同，並且以英漢對照的面貌獨立一冊。周先生似乎獨鍾此書，坊間並未見到他再譯泰氏其他的作品。

一本世界名著，經一譯再譯，先後有多種譯本，這本來是很自然的事，由於隔一段時間，舊的譯本可能已經絕版，或者舊的譯本內容不完全，甚或因爲舊的譯本被認爲水平不佳……等等。尤其最後一個原因，常是後來者決心重譯所持最大的理由。比如上述的糜譯本對於鄭譯本 (諒指初版本) 就有相當不客氣的批評，因此，這也便是促成他下決心重新翻譯的主要動機。

至於我讀了上述四種譯本，當然也免不了有一些感想。按常理

說，後譯者總要比前人進步一些才是，但據本人觀察，事實並不見得如此。比如尙譯本應是最晚的本子，但卻是譯得最糟的一本。鄭氏的譯本雖然出得最早，仍應算是譯得不錯的一本。

江南版的序文中曾說：「泰戈爾的這些短詩，看來並不難譯……但要譯得恰如其意，是不大容易的……」。而我認爲，如果原文看懂了，能否譯得恰如其意，是一回事；但如果原文根本沒有弄懂，譯文又如何能「恰」得起來？茲舉一例，四家譯文 (以出版社代表) 似乎皆顯示沒有讀通原文：

原　文：(CCLV)Find your beauty, my heart, from the world's movement, like the boat that has the grace of the wind and the water.

三民本：我的心，從世界的活動中去尋找你的美麗，像帆船的有風與水之優雅。

晨鐘本：我底心啊，從世界運行中去發現你底美吧，像小艇有風和水底美麗。

普天本：尋覓你的美吧，我的心啊!從這世界的浮動中。宛如那帆船在風與水中的優雅。

江南本：我的心呀，從世界的流動中，找你的美吧，正如那小船得到風與水的優美似的。

這句英文原文整個說起來，實在並不困難，關鍵只在一個字：

grace。以上四家譯文就因爲對這一個字不求甚解，以致把整句中文弄得莫名其妙，尤其後半句，有誰能看得懂它們到底說的什麼？什麼是風與水的優雅？它作爲前半句的比喻又是怎樣比的？

一位嚴肅的翻譯工作者，尤其從事文學翻譯，當然不能靠一般學生所用的袖珍本字典應付，更不能只看頭一個定義，別的都不管了。所謂「優雅」呀，「優美」呀，只不過是grace在字典上的頭一個定義；除此之外，尚有許多其他的意義，如「恩寵、恩惠」等，而由「恩惠」(favor)引伸爲「幫助」(help)。茲根據《韋氏新國際大辭典第三版》(*Webster's Third New International Dictionary*)，對於grace之定義3.d(1)，即爲"an act of kindness, favor"(惠助，幫忙)，並舉例句"do me this grace..."(請幫我個忙)。至於其後所附的成語"by the grace of"更直接解釋爲"with the help of"。是以，grace在本句之中，自以譯爲「助力」較爲恰當，如此全句也就可以說辭暢意達了。下面便是我對這句詩的翻譯：

我的心靈啊，你的美
要在人世的運行中去追尋，
正如帆船的航行，
須靠風和水的助力。

我翻譯《漂鳥集》，同時在形式上也做了一個大膽的嘗試。原來本詩集裏面的詩是不分行的，時常一首詩就只有一句，甚至是很長的一句，而這樣的長句只有在一行排不完時，才轉折到下一行。我國素來的譯者，在形式上大都也就照這個樣子，短句一行，長句也是一行，不管它有多長，除非一行到頁底排不下時，方才轉折到下一行，因此可以說完全不具一般認知中「詩的形式」。而我每讀此詩，心中便有一種衝動，即何妨把它安排得更像詩一點？也就是說，對於原文較長的句子，在翻譯時，視情況 (根據我的直覺) 把它分解成數行排列，使它在形式上看起來讀起來，多增添些許詩的頓挫感——但願泰氏不會反對。另一方面，分行翻譯對於譯文的行文造句，也提供不少方便。茲舉一例，如原詩第二六八首，四家譯文皆顯得拖泥帶水，影響呼吸；若分行譯之，則其糾纏拖沓之弊，可迎刃而解：

原　文：(CCLXVIII) I have learnt the simple meaning of thy whispers in flowers and sunshine—teach me to know thy words in pain and death.

三民本：我已學會在你的花叢中和日光下低語的單純意思
——教我知道你在痛苦與死亡中的語句吧。

晨鐘本：我已明白了你在花和陽光裏低聲訴說的單純意義
——教我了解你痛苦和死亡中的話吧。

普天本：我已學會你在花前與日下喃喃細語的簡單意義。
——教給我了解你在痛苦與死亡中的語言。

江南本：我已學會了你在花與陽光裏微語的意義。
　　——再教我明白你在苦與死中所說的吧。

本　書：您同花和光的喁喁細語，
我已能明白，
它們的意義很單純。
告訴我吧，讓我也明白，
您在痛苦和死亡中
所傾吐的是怎樣的話語。

像這樣把原詩一句分解為若干行 (甚至數句) 翻譯，也許有人會批評：是否違背了「信」的原則？然而，翻譯外國作品，尤其詩歌，誰又能保證「信」到什麼程度？事實上，任何人的翻譯都帶有一定的「創作」成分，因而才有高下優劣之分，不是嗎？近年論翻譯者，有人極力倡導「神似」，而不重「形似」，這是一個趨勢。不過，像我這樣分行翻譯泰氏的《漂鳥集》，對於原作但求「神」似而非常地不求「形」似，這完全是一個個案，一個特例，一項個人的冒險，無論成就如何，並不能成為一個宗派，他人也無由跟進，因為天下並沒有第二位泰戈爾，更沒有第二本*Stray Birds*.

《漂鳥集》到底是怎樣的一個詩集？基本上說，它自然是一個抒情的詩集，其中絕大部分的主題 (雖然全是無題詩，甚至連書名也是取自首篇詩的頭二字) 皆環繞著宇宙間的各種自然現象：花鳥蟲魚，山水草木，日月星辰，天地生死，光明黑暗。不過，因為它也包含部分語錄

式的詩句 (約占百分之十)，內容轉而寄寓人生的哲思哲理，及社會的公理正義，間不乏諷世警世之語，因而使泰氏也贏得詩哲的美譽。書內純抒情詩之清遠雋永，自不需舉示，下面姑就後一類較突出的、較犀利的金句警語，略示數例，且供讀者先睹爲快 (照原詩形式，暫不分行)：

(一五) 別把你的愛置於懸崖絕壁之上，就因為那地方高。

(四五) 將武器視為神明者，當武器戰勝時，他自己便戰敗了。

(六八) 邪惡禁不起考驗，正義卻禁得起。

(一〇八) 如有富貴利達者，誇稱得自上帝的特別恩寵，上帝將感到蒙羞。

(一三〇) 如果你把所有的失誤都關在門外，真理也將被關在門外了。

(二五八) 「錯」永不可能藉權力的增長而變為「對」。

(三一六) 人類的歷史就是耐心的等待，等待那被侮辱者的勝利。

末尾是我講悄悄話的時間。讓我在此獻給我的Better Half，我的財政部長，我的後勤署長，我的「家」策顧問，我的國師同窗爾蘭女士——一句小語：感謝她支持我做了一輩子的書呆子。

本書的出版，承書林出版公司同仁盡心策劃，在版面上力求完美，其任事精神可感，併此致謝。

傅一勤 二〇〇六年二月台北

漂鳥集
Stray Birds

I

Stray birds of summer come to my
window to sing and fly away.
And yellow leaves of autumn, which
have no songs, flutter and fall
there with a sigh.

II

O Troupe of little vagrants of the
world, leave your footprints in
my words.

III

The world puts off its mask of
vastness to its lover.
It becomes small as one song, as
one kiss of the eternal.

IV

It is the tears of the earth that
keep her smiles in bloom.

1

夏天的漂鳥，
飛來我的窗前，
唱支歌，又飛去了。
秋天的黃葉，
沒有歌，只一聲嘆息，
隨風飄落在那兒。

2

世界流浪兒的隊伍啊，
把你們的足跡，
留在我的詩歌裏吧。

3

世界對著它的戀人，
脫下巨大底假面。
它變得渺小，渺如
一支歌，一個永恆底吻。

4

大地因著它的淚水，
使它常保笑容不謝。

V

The mighty desert is burning for the love of a blade of grass who shakes her head and laughs and flies away.

VI

If you shed tears when you miss the sun, you also miss the stars.

VII

The sands in your way beg for your song and your movement, dancing water. Will you carry the burden of their lameness?

VIII

Her wistful face haunts my dreams like the rain at night.

5

廣闊的大漠，
正熱切地渴望著
一片草葉的愛，縱然
草兒只搖一搖頭，
笑一笑，便飛逝了。

6

如果你因為
錯失太陽而流淚，
你也將錯失群星。

7

躺在你途中的泥沙，
乞求你唱支歌流過去，
跳躍的流水啊，
你載得動它們的跛足嗎？

8

她那充滿渴盼的臉容，
不斷縈繞在我的夢中，
宛如夜雨一般。

IX

Once we dreamt that we were strangers.
We wake up to find that we were dear to each other.

X

Sorrow is hushed into peace in my heart like the evening among the silent trees.

XI

Some unseen fingers, like an idle breeze, are playing upon my heart the music of the ripples.

XII

"*What language is thine, O Sea?*"
"*The language of eternal question.*"
"*What language is thy answer, O Sky?*"
"*The language of eternal silence.*"

9

有一次在夢裏，
夢見我們彼此是陌生人。
待醒來卻發現，
我們原是相親相愛的人。

10

我心中的傷痕業已撫平，
平靜得好似林間的黃昏。

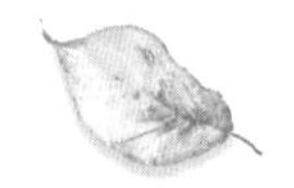

11

看不見是誰的纖指，
像一陣悠悠輕風，
掠過我的心弦，
彈奏著漪波盪漾的旋律。

12

大海啊，
你說的什麼話呀？
——永恆的問。
藍天啊，你答的什麼話呀？
——永恆的沉默。

XIII

Listen, my heart, to the whispers of
the world with which it makes love
to you.

XIV

The mystery of creation is like the
darkness of night—it is great.
Delusions of knowledge are like
the fog of the morning.

XV

Do not seat your love upon a precipice
because it is high.

XVI

I sit at my window this morning where
the world like a passer-by stops for
a moment, nods to me and goes.

13

我的心靈啊，
你聽那世界的低語，
它是在向你示愛呢。

14

造物的奧祕，
有如黑夜之幽深；
知識的幻覺，
彷彿晨間的朝霧。

15

別把你的愛
置於懸崖絕壁之上，
就因為那地方高。

16

今晨坐在窗前，
世界像一位過路人，
在窗前停留片刻，
向我點一點頭，
便又走開了。

XVII

These little thoughts are the rustle of leaves; they have their whisper of joy in my mind.

XVIII

What you are you do not see, what you see is your shadow.

XIX

My wishes are fools, they shout across thy songs, my Master.
Let me but listen.

XX

I cannot choose the best.
The best chooses me.

17

這些零思微想，
宛似林葉間的風聲，
它們在我心底，
吐著歡樂的絮語。

18

真實的你，
你自己看不見，
而你所見的，
只是你的影子。

19

主啊，我的祈願多麼愚蠢，
它衝著您的歌聲嘶喊狂叫。
讓我只靜靜地聆聽吧。

20

我不可能選擇「最佳」；
是「最佳」選擇我。

XXI

They throw their shadows before them who carry their lantern on their back.

XXII

That I exist is a perpetual surprise which is life.

XXIII

"We, the rustling leaves, have a voice that answers the storms, but who are you, so silent?"
"I am a mere flower."

XXIV

Rest belongs to the work as the eyelids to the eyes.

21

把燈籠揹在背後的人，
把身影投在前面。

22

我的存在——
一個永遠的奇蹟，
這就是生命。

23

我們，
蕭蕭的林葉，
用葉聲回答暴風雨，
而你是誰呀，如此沉默？
我只是一朵花。

24

休息之於工作，
猶眼瞼之於眼睛。

XXV

Man is a born child, his power is the power of growth.

XXVI

God expects answers for the flowers he sends us, not for the sun and the earth.

XXVII

The light that plays, like a naked child, among the green leaves happily knows not that man can lie.

XXVIII

O Beauty, find thyself in love, not in the flattery of thy mirror.

25

人如初生的嬰兒，
他的力量，
就是成長的力量。

26

上帝期待我們報答的，
是他送給我們的鮮花，
而不是大地和太陽。

27

陽光如一赤裸的孩子，
只知在綠葉之間嬉戲，
多幸福啊——
卻不知人間的虛偽欺詐。

28

美貌啊，你真實的面目
在你的愛裏，
而不在那諂媚的鏡中。

XXIX

My heart beats her waves at the shore of the world and writes upon it her signature in tears with the words, "I love thee."

XXX

"Moon, for what do you wait?"
"To salute the sun for whom I must make way."

XXXI

The trees come up to my window like the yearning voice of the dumb earth.

XXXII

His own mornings are new surprises to God.

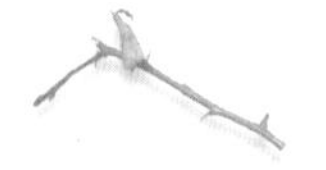

29

我的心如浪潮，
拍擊著世界的海岸，
並用淚水在岸邊留下簽名，
及題字——我愛你。

30

月兒呀，你等待什麼？
等待著禮敬太陽，
我必須給他讓路。

31

綠樹伸頭到我的窗口，
彷彿一種渴望的聲音，
發自瘖啞的大地。

32

上帝所創造的每個清晨，
都使他自己感到新的驚奇。

XXXIII

Life finds its wealth by the claims
of the world, and its worth by the
claims of love.

XXXIV

The dry river-bed finds no thanks
for its past.

XXXV

The bird wishes it were a cloud.
The cloud wishes it were a bird.

XXXVI

The waterfall sings, "I find my song,
when I find my freedom."

33

生命，
由於世人的要求而豐富，
由於愛的要求而產生價值。

34

乾涸的河床，
並不感激它的過去。

35

鳥兒願望是一朵雲。
雲兒願望是一隻鳥。

36

瀑布唱道：
我唱歌的時候，
也就是我找到自由的時候。

XXXVII

I cannot tell why this heart languishes in silence.
It is for small needs it never asks, or knows or remembers.

XXXVIII

Woman, when you move about in your household service, your limbs sing like a hill stream among its pebbles.

XXXIX

The sun goes to cross the Western sea, leaving its last salutation to the East.

XL

Do not blame your food because you have no appetite.

37

我不明白這顆心，
為什麼默然頹喪。
它只是為了某些——
它永遠不問，永遠不懂，
也永遠不會去記憶的，
某些小小需求。

38

女人啊，你來回打理家務，
舉手投足有如潺潺山溪，
輕歌漫舞於溪中小卵石間。

39

太陽滑落西海的海面，
向東方留下最後的敬禮。

40

別因為自己食慾不佳
而責怪食物。

XLI

The trees, like the longings of the earth, stand a-tiptoe to peep at the heaven.

XLII

You smiled and talked to me of nothing and I felt that for this I had been waiting long.

XLIII

The fish in the water is silent, the animal on the earth is noisy, the bird in the air is singing.
But Man has in him the silence of the sea, the noise of the earth and the music of the air.

XLIV

The world rushes on over the strings of the lingering heart making the music of sadness.

41

樹木似大地的渴盼，
踮著足尖向天宇窺覷。

42

你只對著我微笑，
什麼話都不說，
我覺得這情景，
我已等待很久了。

43

水中的游魚默然，
陸上的走獸咆哮，
空中的飛鳥啼鳴。
而人的胸中兼有——
大海的沉默，
大地的喧囂，
天庭的樂章。

44

匆匆的塵世，
衝上彷徨的心弦，
奏著憂鬱的曲調。

XLV

He has made his weapons his gods.
When his weapons win he is defeated himself.

XLVI

God finds himself by creating.

XLVII

Shadow, with her veil drawn, follows Light in secret meekness, with her silent steps of love.

XLVIII

The stars are not afraid to appear like fireflies.

45

將武器視為神明者，
當武器戰勝時，
他自己便戰敗了。

46

上帝創造萬物，
才找到了自己。

47

影子垂下面紗，
秘密地，溫馴地，
跟在「光」的後面，
踏著無聲的愛的腳步。

48

星星不懼自己
螢火蟲的形象。

XLIX

I thank thee that I am none of the wheels of power but I am one with the living creatures that are crushed by it.

L

The mind, sharp but not broad, sticks at every point but does not move.

LI

Your idol is shattered in the dust to prove that God's dust is greater than your idol.

LII

Man does not reveal himself in his history, he struggles up through it.

49

感謝上天，
我沒有做權力的輪子，
而與一切
被權力輾碎的生靈同在。

50

頭腦精明而視野狹小者，
處處執著於細微末節，
而莫知能動。

51

你的偶像
已為塵埃所粉碎，
這適足證明
上帝之塵埃的威力，
遠超越你的偶像。

52

人在一生的過程中，
往往不露痕跡；
他只管埋首奮鬥向上，
走完他的一生。

LIII

While the glass lamp rebukes the earthen for calling it cousin, the moon rises, and the glass lamp, with a bland smile, calls her,—"My dear, dear sister."

LIV

Like the meeting of the seagulls and the waves we meet and come near. The seagulls fly off, the waves roll away and we depart.

LV

My day is done, and I am like a boat drawn on the beach, listening to the dance-music of the tide in the evening.

LVI

Life is given to us, we earn it by giving it.

53

玻璃燈罵瓦燈
沒資格跟它稱兄道弟；
而當月亮升起時，
玻璃燈卻滿臉堆笑，
稱呼月亮——
我親愛的，親愛的姊姊。

54

如同海鷗與海浪，
我們相遇，接近。
海鷗飛去，浪已遠逝，
我們也告別了。

55

我的一天工作完畢。
我像一隻被拖上岸的小舟，
正聆賞著晚潮的舞曲。

56

上天賜予我們生命，
我們必須再給予他人，
方才算是真正得到它。

LVII

We come nearest to the great when we
are great in humility.

LVIII

The sparrow is sorry for the peacock
at the burden of its tail.

LIX

Never be afraid of the moments—thus
sings the voice of the everlasting.

LX

The hurricane seeks the shortest road
by the no-road, and suddenly ends
its search in the Nowhere.

57

我們在卑微時所表現的
偉大，方始近乎偉大。

58

麻雀可憐孔雀有一條
笨重的尾巴。

59

永勿懼怕「剎那」——
此乃「不朽之聲」之歌。

60

颶風在無路處，
尋找最短的捷徑，
又在「烏有鄉」，
驟然終止搜尋。

LXI

Take my wine in my own cup, friend.
It loses its wreath of foam when poured into that of others.

LXII

The Perfect decks itself in beauty for the love of the Imperfect.

LXIII

God says to man, "I heal you, therefore I hurt, love you, therefore punish."

LXIV

Thank the flame for its light, but do not forget the lampholder standing in the shade with constancy of patience.

61

請就著我的杯子，
飲我這杯酒吧，朋友。
倒進他人的杯子，
這一圈酒花便消失了。

62

「完美」因欲博得
「不完美」底愛慕，
而盡量美化自己。

63

上帝對人說：
我能醫治你，故我傷害你；
我愛你，故我罰你。

64

感謝燈火的光明，
但請勿忘記
那挺立在陰影中的燈臺
及其堅定的耐心。

LXV

Tiny grass, your steps are small, but you possess the earth under your tread.

LXVI

The infant flower opens its bud and cries, "Dear World, please do not fade."

LXVII

God grows weary of great kingdoms, but never of little flowers.

LXVIII

Wrong cannot afford defeat but Right can.

65

微渺的小草啊，
你的腳步雖小，
卻擁有你腳下的大地。

66

初露頭角的花兒，
張開它的蓓蕾叫道——
親愛的世界啊，
請您不要凋謝。

67

上帝會厭惡偌大的王國，
卻永不會厭惡一朵小花。

68

邪惡禁不起考驗，
正義卻禁得起。

LXIX

"I give my whole water in joy," sings the waterfall, "though little of it is enough for the thirsty."

LXX

Where is the fountain that throws up these flowers in a ceaseless outbreak of ecstasy?

LXXI

The woodcutter's axe begged for its handle from the tree.
The tree gave it.

LXXII

In my solitude of heart I feel the sigh of this widowed evening veiled with mist and rain.

69

瀑布唱道——
我樂於奉獻我全部的水，
雖然我明白只要一點點，
便足供渴者之需。

70

何處是這噴泉的源頭——
它不斷瘋狂地噴發出
這般水柱銀花？

71

伐木者的利斧，
向樹乞求斧柄。
樹就給它了。

72

寂寥的心情，
使我體會到這失偶的黃昏，
獨處在濛濛煙雨下的嘆息。

LXXIII

Chastity is a wealth that comes from abundance of love.

LXXIV

The mist, like love, plays upon the heart of the hills and brings out surprises of beauty.

LXXV

We read the world wrong and say that it deceives us.

LXXVI

The poet wind is out over the sea and the forest to seek his own voice.

73

貞潔這項財富，
出自豐盈的愛。

74

朝霧如似愛神，
流連在群山的懷抱，
變幻出奇異的美景。

75

我們誤解了世界，
反說它欺騙了我們。

76

如詩人般的風，
掠過海洋和山林，
去追尋它自己的聲音。

LXXVII

Every child comes with the message that God is not yet discouraged of man.

LXXVIII

The grass seeks her crowd in the earth.
The tree seeks his solitude of the sky.

LXXIX

Man barricades against himself.

LXXX

Your voice, my friend, wanders in my heart, like the muffled sound of the sea among these listening pines.

77

每個嬰孩都帶來一項信息：
上帝對世人尚未失望。

78

小草在土中尋覓夥伴；
大樹向天空追求孤獨。

79

人常架設起路障，
堵住自己的去路。

80

我的朋友，
你的聲音迴盪在我心底，
彷彿隱隱的海潮聲，
盤旋在這傾聽的松林。

LXXXI

What is this unseen flame of darkness whose sparks are the stars?

LXXXII

Let life be beautiful like summer flowers and death like autumn leaves.

LXXXIII

He who wants to do good knocks at the gate; he who loves finds the gate open.

LXXXIV

In death the many becomes one; in life the one becomes many.
Religion will be one when God is dead.

81

這不見光焰的黑暗之火，
它到底是什麼樣的火——
它的火花，
不就是天上的繁星嗎？

82

但願——
生命美如夏日的鮮花，
死亡美如秋天的紅葉。

83

欲行善者，必須敲門；
獻愛心者，大門為之敞開。

84

人死後大眾歸「一」；
活著「一」生大眾。
上帝死了，
宗教歸一。

LXXXV

The artist is the lover of Nature, therefore he is her slave and her master.

LXXXVI

"How far are you from me, O Fruit?"
"I am hidden in your heart, O Flower."

LXXXVII

This longing is for the one who is felt in the dark, but not seen in the day.

LXXXVIII

"You are the big drop of dew under the lotus leaf, I am the smaller one on its upper side," said the dewdrop to the lake.

85

藝術家乃大自然的戀人，
因此，他是大自然的奴隸，
也是大自然的主人。

86

果兒啊，
你離我有多遠？
花兒啊，
我就躲在你的心窩裏。

87

這一分渴念只為一個人，
在黑夜裏我能感覺到他，
雖在白天看不見他。

88

露珠對湖水說：
你是荷葉底下的大露珠，
我是荷葉上面的小露珠。

LXXXIX

The scabbard is content to be dull when
it protects the keenness of the sword.

XC

In darkness the One appears as uniform;
in the light the One appears as
manifold.

XCI

The great earth makes herself hospitable
with the help of the grass.

XCII

The birth and death of the leaves are
the rapid whirls of the eddy whose
wider circles move slowly among stars.

89

劍鞘雖有責保護劍鋒的利，
卻滿足於自身的鈍。

90

所謂「太一」，
在黑暗中狀似一統。
所謂「太一」，
在光明中則呈現多元。

91

遼闊無垠的大地，
由於小草的幫助，
給予萬物一可居之所。

92

木葉的生生滅滅，
猶如一疾速的漩渦中心，
而漩渦的外緣，
則緩緩運行於星辰之間。

XCIII

Power said to the world, "You are mine."
The world kept it prisoner on her throne.
Love said to the world, "I am thine."
The world gave it the freedom of her house.

XCIV

The mist is like the earth's desire.
It hides the sun for whom she cries.

XCV

Be still, my heart, these great trees are prayers.

XCVI

The noise of the moment scoffs at the music of the Eternal.

93

權力對世界說：
你是屬於我的。
於是世界把權力，
囚禁在她的寶座旁。
愛對世界說：
我是屬於您的。
於是世界便讓愛，
自由出入她的寶殿。

94

雲霧彷彿大地的慾望，
它遮蔽了
大地所渴求的太陽。

95

肅靜吧，我的心靈，
這些大樹正在做祈禱呢。

96

瞬間的喧嘩，
嘲笑永恆底音樂。

XCVII

I think of other ages that floated upon the stream of life and love and death and are forgotten, and I feel the freedom of passing away.

XCVIII

The sadness of my soul is her bride's veil.
It waits to be lifted in the night.

XCIX

Death's stamp gives value to the coin of life; making it possible to buy with life what is truly precious.

C

The cloud stood humbly in a corner of the sky.
The morning crowned it with splendour.

97

想起過往的世世代代，
漂過生、愛、死的洪流，
然後被遺忘——
我體悟到棄世的自由。

98

我靈魂的愁苦，
如同新娘的面紗，
要等到深夜才得揭起。

99

死亡給生命之幣烙上面值；
如此方才可能，用生命
去購買真正的無價之寶。

100

一朵白雲謙卑地
立在天空的一角。
晨曦用壯麗的色彩
來給它加冕。

CI

The dust receives insult and in return offers her flowers.

CII

Do not linger to gather flowers to keep them, but walk on, for flowers will keep themselves blooming all your way.

CIII

Roots are the branches down in the earth.
Branches are roots in the air.

CIV

The music of the far-away summer flutters around the autumn seeking its former nest.

101

塵土忍受屈辱，
卻回報以鮮花。

102

別停下來採集道旁的花朵；
只管向前走吧，
花兒將跟隨你的腳步，
沿路不斷開放。

103

根是地下的枝；
枝是空中的根。

104

遠去的夏日之聲，
仍在秋之四野飄蕩，
尋覓它的舊巢。

CV

Do not insult your friend by lending him merits from your own pocket.

CVI

The touch of the nameless days clings to my heart like mosses round the old tree.

CVII

The echo mocks her origin to prove she is the original.

CVIII

God is ashamed when the prosperous boasts of his special favour.

105

別掏腰包替朋友充面子，
這對他是一種羞辱。

106

提起那些莫名的日子，
一種感觸便附著在我心頭，
猶如攀緣在古樹上的青苔。

107

回音偽裝原音，
妄圖魚目混珠。

108

如有富貴利達者，
誇稱得自上帝的特別恩寵，
上帝將感到蒙羞。

CIX

I cast my own shadow upon my path,
because I have a lamp that has not been lighted.

CX

Man goes into the noisy crowd to drown his own clamour of silence.

CXI

That which ends in exhaustion is death, but the perfect ending is in the endless.

CXII

The sun has his simple robe of light. The clouds are decked with gorgeousness.

109

我的影子投射在路中央，
因為我的燈沒有點燃。

110

人走入喧囂的群眾，
以淹沒其沉默底吶喊。

111

因耗盡而盡，即是死亡，
而最完美的盡，則是無盡。

112

太陽只有一襲樸素的光袍，
雲霞則穿著絢麗的彩服。

CXIII

The hills are like shouts of children who raise their arms, trying to catch stars.

CXIV

The road is lonely in its crowd, for it is not loved.

CXV

The power that boasts of its mischiefs is laughed at by the yellow leaves that fall, and clouds that pass by.

CXVI

The earth hums to me to-day in the sun, like a woman at her spinning, some ballad of the ancient time in a forgotten tongue.

113

青山如一群叫嚷的孩子，
他們高舉雙手，
企圖去捕捉天上的星星。

114

路上的行人雖多，
路是寂寞的，
因為它沒有得到愛。

115

權力在誇耀它的罪惡時，
為凋零的黃葉所嘲弄，
為過往的白雲所譏笑。

116

今天，大地在太陽下，
對我哼著一曲古民謠，
玄古的歌詞不知說些什麼，
宛如一位村婦，
搖著她碌碌的紡車。

CXVII

The grass-blade is worthy of the great
world where it grows.

CXVIII

Dream is a wife who must talk.
Sleep is a husband who silently suffers.

CXIX

The night kisses the fading day whispering
to his ear, "I am death, your mother.
I am to give you fresh birth."

CXX

I feel thy beauty, dark night, like that
of the loved woman when she has put
out the lamp.

117

一片草葉，無愧於
它所生長的大世界。

118

夢是妻，只管喋喋不休；
眠是夫，惟有默默忍受。

119

夜吻著殘晝低聲道：
我乃死亡，你的母親，
我將予你新生。

120

黑漆漆的夜啊，我覺得
你的美很像一位情婦，
美在滅燈以後。

CXXI

I carry in my world that flourishes the worlds that have failed.

CXXII

Dear friend, I feel the silence of your great thoughts of many a deepening eventide on this beach when I listen to these waves.

CXXIII

The bird thinks it is an act of kindness to give the fish a lift in the air.

CXXIV

"In the moon thou sendest thy love letters to me," said the night to the sun.
"I leave my answers in tears upon the grass."

121

我在這繁盛昌隆的世界裏，
肩負著諸多傾頹的世界。

122

親愛的朋友，每當我
聆聽著這海灘的濤聲，
就體會到你對這兒
多少暮色漸濃的黃昏，
所懷無比沉默的思念。

123

鳥兒認為，
把水中的魚兒抓入空中，
乃是一項善行。

124

夜對太陽說：
您拜託月亮把您的情書，
交給了我。
我把我的答覆：淚水，
留在草葉上。

CXXV

The Great is a born child; when he dies
he gives his great childhood to the
world.

CXXVI

Not hammer-strokes, but dance of the
water sings the pebbles into perfection.

CXXVII

Bees sip honey from flowers and hum their
thanks when they leave.
The gaudy butterfly is sure that the flowers
owe thanks to him.

CXXVIII

To be outspoken is easy when you do not
wait to speak the complete truth.

125

偉人生就只是個孩子，
死後便把他的偉大童年，
留給世人。

126

不是由於鐵鎚的敲打，
而是由於載歌載舞的流水，
把溪中的小石子，
琢磨得如此玲瓏完美。

127

蜜蜂採完花蜜離開時，
一聲嗡鳴，表示道謝。
艷麗的蝴蝶相信，
花應該向牠道謝。

128

直言快語並不難，
只要你不想等到那一刻，
能夠說出全然的真理。

CXXIX

Asks the Possible of the Impossible,
"Where is your dwelling-place?"
"In the dreams of the impotent,"
comes the answer.

CXXX

If you shut your door to all errors
truth will be shut out.

CXXXI

I hear some rustle of things behind
my sadness of heart,—I cannot
see them.

CXXXII

Leisure in its activity is work.
The stillness of the sea stirs in waves.

129

「可能」問「不可能」道：
你的住所在何處？
對方答道：
在無能者的幻夢中。

130

如果你把所有的失誤
都關在門外，
真理也將被關在門外了。

131

在我傷心的背後，
我聽見有物沙沙作響——
只是我看不見它們。

132

休閒之時，
活動起來即是工作。
靜止的海水，
翻攪起來便成波濤。

CXXXIII

The leaf becomes flower when it loves.
The flower becomes fruit when it worships.

CXXXIV

The roots below the earth claim no rewards for making the branches fruitful.

CXXXV

This rainy evening the wind is restless.
I look at the swaying branches and ponder over the greatness of all things.

CXXXVI

Storm of midnight, like a giant child awakened in the untimely dark, has begun to play and shout.

133

葉因有愛而開花。
花因敬天而結果。

134

泥土下面的根，
營養枝幹結實纍纍，
並不要求任何報酬。

135

雨濛濛的黃昏，
風也吹個不停。
我仰望著搖曳的樹木，
沉思萬物的偉大。

136

午夜的暴風雨，
像個孩子巨人，
在莫名的黑暗中被喚醒，
開始戲耍吼叫起來。

CXXXVII

Thou raisest thy waves vainly to follow thy lover, O sea, thou lonely bride of the storm.

CXXXVIII

"I am ashamed of my emptiness," said the Word to the Work.
"I know how poor I am when I see you," said the Work to the Word.

CXXXIX

Time is the wealth of change, but the clock in its parody makes it mere change and no wealth.

CXL

Truth in her dress finds facts too tight.
In fiction she moves with ease.

137

大海啊，
你這位孤零零的
暴風雨底新娘，
徒然掀起萬頃波濤，
去追逐你的情郎。

138

文字對工作說：
我很慚愧，我很空虛。
工作對文字說：
一見到你，我就知道，
我是多麼貧乏。

139

時間是「變」的寶庫；
時鐘不過假扮時間的小丑，
故只有「變」，沒有寶庫。

140

真理穿起真理之服，
感覺「世事」綁手縛足。
但在虛構故事中，
真理卻活動自如。

CXLI

When I travelled to here and to there,
I was tired of thee, O Road, but now
when thou leadest me to everywhere
I am wedded to thee in love.

CXLII

Let me think that there is one among
those stars that guides my life through
the dark unknown.

CXLIII

Woman, with the grace of your fingers
you touched my things and order came
out like music.

CXLIV

One sad voice has its nest among the
ruins of the years.
It sings to me in the night,—"I loved
you."

141

從前我浪跡四方，
東奔西走，漫無目的，
路啊，我煩厭過你。
而今，你引導著我
走遍天涯海角，
我與你已結為愛的一體了。

142

我好想在那繁星之中
正有一顆，
來指引著我的一生，
走過不可知的黑暗。

143

女人啊，
你以纖纖玉指隨意撥弄一下，
我的一切都變得井然有序了，
美得像一首樂曲。

144

一個淒涼的聲音，
巢居在那千年的廢墟中。
它在深夜裏向我唱著——
我愛過你。

CXLV

The flaming fire warns me off by its own glow.
Save me from the dying embers hidden under ashes.

CXLVI

I have my stars in the sky, but oh for my little lamp unlit in my house.

CXLVII

The dust of the dead words clings to thee.
Wash thy soul with silence.

CXLVIII

Gaps are left in life through which comes the sad music of death.

145

正燃燒中的火焰，
有紅光警告我勿靠近它。
誰來救我呀，使我遠離那
埋藏在灰燼下面的餘火？

146

我已擁有滿天的星斗，
然而，唉，我仍思念著
我室內未燃的小燈。

147

死去的文字，
化為塵土沾滿你一身。
用沉默洗淨你的靈魂吧。

148

生命裏留下許多罅隙，
由此漏出死亡的哀樂。

CXLIX

The world has opened its heart of light in the morning.
Come out, my heart, with thy love to meet it.

CL

My thoughts shimmer with these shimmering leaves and my heart sings with the touch of this sunlight; my life is glad to be floating with all things into the blue of space, into the dark of time.

CLI

God's great power is in the gentle breeze, not in the storm.

CLII

This is a dream in which things are all loose and they oppress. I shall find them gathered in thee when I awake and shall be free.

149

世界一大清早
就敞開了它的光明之心。
我的心靈啊，你也走出來，
帶著愛去迎接它吧。

150

我的思緒，
隨著閃爍的綠葉閃爍。
我的心靈，
隨著陽光的輕撫而歡唱。
我的生命，
願隨萬物
漂入太空的穹藍，
沉入時間的深淵。

151

上帝的大力量，
展現在輕柔的微風裏，
而不在狂風暴雨中。

152

這簡直是一場惡夢，
萬物都跑出來壓迫著我。
願醒來發現，一切都已為您收拾去，
還我自由。

CLIII

"Who is there to take up my duties?"
asked the setting sun.
"I shall do what I can, my Master,"
said the earthen lamp.

CLIV

By plucking her petals you do not
gather the beauty of the flower.

CLV

Silence will carry your voice like the
nest that holds the sleeping birds.

CLVI

The Great walks with the Small without
fear.
The Middling keeps aloof.

153

落日問道：
有誰來接替我的職務？
瓦燈答道：
我將盡我所能，主人。

154

摘下一片片花瓣，
你採不到花的美。

155

沉默能載住你的聲音，
猶如鳥巢能載住睡鳥。

156

偉大者不懼與渺小者同行；
居中者卻避而遠之。

CLVII

*The night opens the flowers in secret
and allows the day to get thanks.*

CLVIII

*Power takes as ingratitude the writhings
of its victims.*

CLIX

*When we rejoice in our fullness, then
we can part with our fruits with joy.*

CLX

*The raindrops kissed the earth and
whispered,—"We are thy homesick
children, mother, come back to thee
from the heaven."*

157

黑夜秘助百花開放，
卻讓白晝領受感謝。

158

權力視受害者的痛苦掙扎
為忘恩負義。

159

當我們歡慶成長成熟時，
便會樂意甩下我們的果實。

160

小雨點兒吻著大地低訴道：
母親啊，
我們都是好想家的孩子，
現自天宮又回到您的懷裏來了。

CLXI

The cobweb pretends to catch dewdrops and catches flies.

CLXII

Love! When you come with the burning lamp of pain in your hand, I can see your face and know you as bliss.

CLXIII

"The learned say that your lights will one day be no more," said the firefly to the stars.
The stars made no answer.

CLXIV

In the dusk of the evening the bird of some early dawn comes to the nest of my silence.

161

蛛網假意捕捉露珠，
卻捉住蒼蠅。

162

愛情啊！
你手持燃著痛苦的燈而來，
但我看得見你的容顏，
認得你乃是天賜至福。

163

螢火蟲對星星說：
是學者們說的，
你們的光有一天會消滅。
星星沒有回答。

164

暮色蒼茫中，
一隻他日的黎明之鳥，
飛入我的沉默之巢。

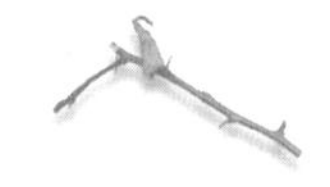

CLXV

Thoughts pass in my mind like flocks of ducks in the sky.
I hear the voice of their wings.

CLXVI

The canal loves to think that rivers exist solely to supply it with water.

CLXVII

The world has kissed my soul with its pain, asking for its return in songs.

CLXVIII

That which oppresses me, is it my soul trying to come out in the open, or the soul of the world knocking at my heart for its entrance?

165

縷縷思緒飄過我的腦際，
彷彿空中飛過的雁陣。
我聽見牠們的鼓翼聲。

166

酷愛遐思的運河，
以為百川的存在，
只是為了供應運河之水。

167

世界帶著痛苦來吻我的靈魂，
懇求我以詩歌為報。

168

那壓迫著我的——
是我的靈魂
掙扎著要走出曠野？
還是世界的靈魂
叩著我的心扉要求進入？

CLXIX

Thought feeds itself with its own words
and grows.

CLXX

I have dipped the vessel of my heart
into this silent hour; it has filled
with love.

CLXXI

Either you have work or you have not.
When you have to say, "Let us do something,"
then begins mischief.

CLXXII

The sunflower blushed to own the nameless
flower as her kin.
The sun rose and smiled on it, saying,
"Are you well, my darling?"

169

思想用它自己的語言，
營養自己，成長茁壯。

170

我將心靈的水瓶，
浸入這萬籟俱寂的時刻，
汲了一滿瓶的愛。

171

不管你此刻
有工作，還是沒有。
一旦你感到不得不說：
「讓我們想個法子吧」
小麻煩便開始活動了。

172

向日葵羞於承認
無名小花是她的親戚。
太陽出來了，
卻笑著向無名小花說：
親愛的，你好嗎？

CLXXIII

"Who drives me forward like fate?"
"The Myself striding on my back."

CLXXIV

The clouds fill the water-cups of the river, hiding themselves in the distant hills.

CLXXV

I spill water from my water-jar as I walk on my way.
Very little remains for my home.

CLXXVI

The water in a vessel is sparkling; the water in the sea is dark.
The small truth has words that are clear; the great truth has great silence.

173

是誰，像命運一般，
驅策著我向前？
原是那跨在我背脊上的
「自我」啊。

174

雲兒注滿河川的水杯，
卻把自己隱藏在遠山裏。

175

我提著一滿瓶水，
一路上潑潑灑灑，
只剩下很少攜回家中。

176

盤中之水浮光閃閃；
海中之水一片黝黑。
小道理其理易明；
大道理惟見大默。

CLXXVII

Your smile was the flowers of your own fields, your talk was the rustle of your own mountain pines, but your heart was the woman that we all know.

CLXXVIII

It is the little things that I leave behind for my loved ones,—great things are for everyone.

CLXXIX

Woman, thou hast encircled the world's heart with the depth of thy tears as the sea has the earth.

CLXXX

The sunshine greets me with a smile.
The rain, his sad sister, talks to my heart.

177

你的笑容，
是你田裏的花朵；
你的談吐，
是你山林的松聲；
而你的心，
卻如世間的婦人一般。

178

我把小的東西，
留給我親愛的人，
大的東西留給大家。

179

女人啊，
您以似海深的淚水，
環抱著世界的心，
一如海洋環抱著大地。

180

陽光，
以微笑向我問好。
小雨點兒，太陽的苦妹，
跟我談心。

CLXXXI

My flower of the day dropped its petals forgotten.
In the evening it ripens into a golden fruit of memory.

CLXXXII

I am like the road in the night listening to the footfalls of its memories in silence.

CLXXXIII

The evening sky to me is like a window, and a lighted lamp, and a waiting behind it.

CLXXXIV

He who is too busy doing good finds no time to be good.

181

我的白日之花，
花瓣凋謝，便被遺忘了。
黃昏時，花心中間
卻結出一粒記憶底金果。

182

我像深夜的大路，
正靜靜地傾聽著，
自己記憶底足音。

183

黃昏的天空，
對我像一扇窗，
一盞點亮的燈，
跟那燈後的等待。

184

過份忙於行善者，
往往無暇修身養性。

CLXXXV

I am the autumn cloud, empty of rain,
see my fullness in the field of
ripened rice.

CLXXXVI

They hated and killed and men praised
them.
But God in shame hastens to hide its
memory under the green grass.

CLXXXVII

Toes are the fingers that have forsaken
their past.

CLXXXVIII

Darkness travels towards light, but
blindness towards death.

185

我是空空的秋雲，
雨水已盡，
但見田野一片稻熟，
那便是我的滿足。

186

憎恨，殺戮，
受到世人稱頌。
上帝甚覺羞慚，
忙把記憶埋藏在綠草底下。

187

足趾乃是
背棄其「過去」的手指。

188

黑暗走向光明；
盲目走向死亡。

CLXXXIX

The pet dog suspects the universe for scheming to take its place.

CXC

Sit still, my heart, do not raise your dust.
Let the world find its way to you.

CXCI

The bow whispers to the arrow before it speeds forth—"Your freedom is mine."

CXCII

Woman, in your laughter you have the music of the fountain of life.

189

受人類寵愛的小狗，
猜疑宇宙
陰謀奪取牠的地位。

190

靜靜地坐著吧，
我的心靈啊，
別揚起你的塵土；
讓世界循它自己的路，
來找到你。

191

弓對弦上待發的箭低聲說：
你的自由就是我的自由。

192

女人啊，
在你的笑聲裏
藏著生命之泉的音樂。

CXCIII

A mind all logic is like a knife all blade.
It makes the hand bleed that uses it.

CXCIV

God loves man's lamp-lights better than his own great stars.

CXCV

This world is the world of wild storms kept tame with the music of beauty.

CXCVI

"My heart is like the golden casket of thy kiss," said the sunset cloud to the sun.

193

一顆滿是「邏輯」的頭腦，
有如一把多刃的刀，
它會割傷使用者的手。

194

上帝愛人間的燈火，
勝於愛他自己的巨星。

195

這是個充滿風雨的世界，
幸而一切狂風暴雨
皆為美底音樂所馴服。

196

晚霞對落日說：
我的心好似一金匣，
裏面盡藏著您的吻。

CXCVII

By touching you may kill, by keeping away you may possess.

CXCVIII

The cricket's chirp and the patter of rain come to me through the dark, like the rustle of dreams from my past youth.

CXCIX

"I have lost my dewdrop," cries the flower to the morning sky that has lost all its stars.

CC

The burning log bursts in flame and cries, —"This is my flower, my death."

197

觸到它你可能毀掉它；
遠離它則可能擁有它。

198

蟋蟀的鳴聲，
夜雨的淅瀝聲，
從黑暗中向我耳邊飄來——
彷彿是我那久已逝去的
青春之夢的交響曲。

199

清晨的晴空，
失落了滿天的星斗；
花兒向天空嚷道：
我失落了我的露珠。

200

燃燒的木頭，
迸出一團火焰，叫道：
這是我的花朵，
　　我的死亡。

CCI

The wasp thinks that the honey-hive of
the neighbouring bees is too small.
His neighbours ask him to build one
still smaller.

CCII

"I cannot keep your waves," says the
bank to the river.
"Let me keep your footprints in my
heart."

CCIII

The day, with the noise of this little
earth, drowns the silence of all worlds.

CCIV

The song feels the infinite in the air,
the picture in the earth,
the poem in the air and the earth;
For its words have meaning that walks
and music that soars.

201

大黃蜂正想著隔鄰
小蜜蜂的蜂巢太小。
小蜜蜂卻央求牠
幫築一個更小的。

202

河岸對河水說：
我保存不住你的波浪。
讓我把你的足跡
保存在我心裏吧。

203

白晝圖以小小地球的喧嚷，
淹沒全宇宙的默然。

歌聲感到天空的無限，
繪畫感到大地的無限，
詩感到天和地的無限。
因為詩的語言，
有靈動的意義，
和翱翔的音樂。

CCV

When the sun goes down to the West, the East of his morning stands before him in silence.

CCVI

Let me not put myself wrongly to my world and set it against me.

CCVII

Praise shames me, for I secretly beg for it.

CCVIII

Let my doing nothing when I have nothing to do become untroubled in its depth of peace like the evening in the seashore when the water is silent.

205

太陽墜落西山時，
東方擁著晨曦，
悄立在它的前面。

206

別讓我有負於世界，
而使它不利於我。

207

讚美使我有些害羞，
因我竊喜求之不得。

208

讓我在因無為而無為時，
不要受到干擾，
那份深深的寧靜，
一若黃昏無波的海濱。

CCIX

Maiden, your simplicity, like the blueness of the lake, reveals your depth of truth.

CCX

The best does not come alone.
It comes with the company of the all.

CCXI

God's right hand is gentle, but terrible is his left hand.

CCXII

My evening came among the alien trees and spoke in a language which my morning stars did not know.

209

年輕的女郎啊，
你的質樸似湖水的湛藍，
透露出無盡的純真。

210

「最佳之福」不獨行；
它會隨著萬事萬物而來。

211

上帝的右臂溫和，
左臂嚴酷。

212

我的夕陽黃昏，
來到奇異的林間，
説著垂暮的語言，
讓曉星理解也難。

CCXIII

Night's darkness is a bag that bursts
with the gold of the dawn.

CCXIV

Our desire lends the colours of the rainbow
to the mere mists and vapours of life.

CCXV

God waits to win back his own flowers as
gifts from man's hands.

CCXVI

My sad thoughts tease me asking me
their own names.

213

深夜的無邊黑暗恰似一布袋，
袋內即將爆發出黎明的金光。

214

人之慾望僅給生命的雲煙，
平添些許彩虹的顏色。

215

上帝期待著，
從獻花人的手中，
收回原屬他自己的鮮花。

216

我的愁思戲問我——
它們叫什麼名字？

CCXVII

The service of the fruit is precious,
the service of the flower is sweet,
but let my service be the service of
the leaves in its shade of humble devotion.

CCXVIII

My heart has spread its sails to the
idle winds for the shadowy island
of Anywhere.

CCXIX

Men are cruel, but Man is kind.

CCXX

Make me thy cup and let my fullness
be for thee and for thine.

217

果實的奉獻是珍貴的，
花的奉獻是甜美的，
而我只想做卑微的樹葉，
奉獻一片綠蔭。

218

我的心靈的船，
揚起船帆，迎著懶懶的風，
航向那天涯海角的奇幻島。

219

群眾是殘忍的，
但每個人都是善良的。

220

讓我做您的酒杯吧，
把我斟滿，
獻給您和屬於您的人。

CCXXI

The storm is like the cry of some god in pain whose love the earth refuses.

CCXXII

The world does not leak because death is not a crack.

CCXXIII

Life has become richer by the love that has been lost.

CCXXIV

My friend, your great heart shone with the sunrise of the East like the snowy summit of a lonely hill in the dawn.

221

暴風雨彷彿是
某位天神的痛苦呼號，
只因為大地拒絕了他的愛。

222

世界是堅固不漏的，
因為死亡並不會
造成任何裂隙。

223

生命因為失去愛，
而變得更豐富。

224

朋友，你的偉大的心靈，
隨著東升旭日閃閃發光，
宛若天色微明中的白雪孤峰。

CCXXV

The fountain of death makes the still water of life play.

CCXXVI

Those who have everything but thee, my God, laugh at those who have nothing but thyself.

CCXXVII

The movement of life has its rest in its own music.

CCXXVIII

Kicks only raise dust and not crops from the earth.

225

死亡如一噴泉，
它促使生命的止水
復活。

226

我的上帝啊，
那些擁有一切而沒有您之人，
嘲笑一無所有而擁有您之人。

227

生命的運動，
在它自己的音樂中，
得到休憩。

228

用足蹴地只能揚起塵土，
不能使地裏長出禾麥來。

CCXXIX

Our names are the light that flows on the sea waves at night and then dies without leaving its signature.

CCXXX

Let him only see the thorns who has eyes to see the rose.

CCXXXI

Set the bird's wings with gold and it will never again soar in the sky.

CCXXXII

The same lotus of our clime blooms here in the alien water with the same sweetness, under another name.

229

我人的名姓，
不過深夜海上的波光，
傾刻間消逝無蹤，
也不留下一個簽字。

230

讓那有眼觀賞玫瑰花的人，
只看見它的刺。

231

給鳥兒兩隻鑲金的翅翼，
它再也不能翱翔天際了。

232

跟我家鄉同樣的荷花，
在這異域的水中綻放，
一樣芳香，兩樣名堂。

CCXXXIII

In heart's perspective the distance looms large.

CCXXXIV

The moon has her light all over the sky, her dark spots to herself.

CCXXXV

Do not say, "It is morning," and dismiss it with a name of yesterday. See it for the first time as a new-born child that has no name.

CCXXXVI

Smoke boasts to the sky, and Ashes to the earth, that they are brothers to the fire.

233

在心靈的透視線上，
遠處反而顯得迫近眼前。

234

月兒光披滿天，
卻把黑斑留給自己。

235

別只說一聲「這是清晨」，
便匆匆棄之如昨日事。
仔細瞧瞧它吧，如同
初見一尚未命名的新生兒。

236

青煙向天空誇耀，
死灰向大地誇耀，
自稱都是火的兄弟。

CCXXXVII

The raindrop whispered to the jasmine,
"Keep me in your heart for ever."
The jasmine sighed, "Alas," and dropped
to the ground.

CCXXXVIII

Timid thoughts, do not be afraid of me.
I am a poet.

CCXXXIX

The dim silence of my mind seems filled
with crickets' chirp—the grey twilight
of sound.

CCXL

Rockets, your insult to the stars follows
yourself back to the earth.

237

雨點兒向茉莉花耳語道：
把我永遠藏在你心底吧。
茉莉花一聲嘆息：唉！
便墜落地上。

238

羞怯的思緒啊，
別怕我，
我是一位詩人。

239

我的心中一片寧靜，
朦朧間似聽見蟋蟀聲——
一種微弱聲音的曙光。

240

沖天的火箭啊，
你對星星的無禮，
跟隨你又回到地球上來了。

CCXLI

Thou hast led me through my crowded travels of the day to my evening's loneliness.
I wait for its meaning through the stillness of the night.

CCXLII

This life is the crossing of a sea, where we meet in the same narrow ship.
In death we reach the shore and go to our different worlds.

CCXLIII

The stream of truth flows through its channels of mistakes.

CCXLIV

My heart is homesick to-day for the one sweet hour across the sea of time.

241

您引導著我
走完一天擁擠的旅程，
日暮獨向黃昏。
我等待深夜的靜寂，
讓我體會孤獨底意義。

242

人生如渡海，
大家相遇在同一狹窄的舟中；
死亡迎我們同登彼岸，
然後又奔向各自的世界。

243

真理的河川，
由錯誤底支流匯集而成。

244

今天心裏忽興起鄉愁，
渴望渡過時間的大海，
去尋覓那甜蜜的一刻。

CCXLV

The bird-song is the echo of the morning light back from the earth.

CCXLVI

"*Are you too proud to kiss me?*" *the morning light asks the buttercup.*

CCXLVII

"*How may I sing to thee and worship, O Sun?*" *asked the little flower.*
"*By the simple silence of thy purity,*" *answered the sun.*

CCXLVIII

Man is worse than an animal when he is an animal.

245

鳥兒的歌聲
是晨光照耀在大地上
所反射的回音。

246

晨光問金鳳花：
你是否因為太高傲
不屑來吻我？

247

小花問道：太陽啊，
我該怎樣歌唱來崇拜您呢？
太陽答道：很簡單，
只要用你純潔底無聲。

248

當人只是動物時，
比動物更不如。

CCXLIX

*Dark clouds become heaven's flowers
when kissed by light.*

CCL

*Let not the sword-blade mock its handle
for being blunt.*

CCLI

*The night's silence, like a deep lamp,
is burning with the light of its
Milky Way.*

CCLII

*Around the sunny island of life swells
day and night death's limitless song
of the sea.*

249

烏雲只為陽光一吻，
便成為天上的奇葩。

250

莫讓劍刃，
嘲笑劍柄鈍。

251

夜之無邊的寂靜，
彷彿一盞幽深的巨燈，
燃燒著銀河的星光。

252

生命如一陽光普照的孤島，
大海日夜在它四周，
咆哮著無盡的死亡之歌。

CCLIII

Is not this mountain like a flower, with its petals of hills, drinking the sunlight?

CCLIV

The real with its meaning read wrong and emphasis misplaced is the unreal.

CCLV

Find your beauty, my heart, from the world's movement, like the boat that has the grace of the wind and the water.

CCLVI

The eyes are not proud of their sight but of their eyeglasses.

253

這座高山很像一朵花，
小丘陵便是它的花瓣，
它們正一同吸吮著陽光呢，
——你說不是嗎？

254

如果「真實」的
意義被誤解，
輕重被倒置，
便是「非真實」。

255

我的心靈啊，你的美
要在人世的運行中去追尋，
正如帆船的航行，
須靠風和水的助力。

256

眼睛，不以視力傲人，
卻以所戴的眼鏡傲人。

CCLVII

I live in this little world of mine and am afraid to make it the least less. Lift me into thy world and let me have the freedom gladly to lose my all.

CCLVIII

The false can never grow into truth by growing in power.

CCLIX

My heart, with its lapping waves of song, longs to caress this green world of the sunny day.

CCLX

Wayside grass, love the star, then your dreams will come out in flowers.

257

我住在我的小小世界裏，
尤恐其有愈來愈小之勢。
救我到您的世界裏來吧，
我甘願喪失我的一切。

258

「錯」永不可能
藉權力的增長而變為「對」。

259

我的心靈之歌，
有如水面上的漣漪，
渴望輕輕一擁
這陽光和煦的綠色世界。

260

路邊的小草啊，
只要你愛那顆星星，
你的夢就會開出花來。

CCLXI

Let your music, like a sword, pierce the noise of the market to its heart.

CCLXII

The trembling leaves of this tree touch my heart like the fingers of an infant child.

CCLXIII

The little flower lies in the dust.
It sought the path of the butterfly.

CCLXIV

I am in the world of the roads.
The night comes. Open thy gate, thou world of the home.

261

讓你的音樂像一把利劍，
對準那鼎沸的市井之聲，
直刺入它的心臟。

262

樹在風中顫抖的枯葉，
宛似初生嬰兒的指尖，
觸動我的心弦。

263

小花躺在塵土裏，
尋覓蝴蝶飛舞的路徑。

264

我正徘徊在
「路」的世界中。
黑夜來臨了，
請打開您的大門吧，
您這「家」的世界。

CCLXV

I have sung the songs of thy day.
In the evening let me carry thy lamp through the stormy path.

CCLXVI

I do not ask thee into the house.
Come into my infinite loneliness, my Lover.

CCLXVII

Death belongs to life as birth does.
The walk is in the raising of the foot as in the laying of it down.

CCLXVIII

I have learnt the simple meaning of thy whispers in flowers and sunshine—teach me to know thy words in pain and death.

265

我已唱過了
您的白日之歌。
晚上讓我攜著您的燈，
穿過那風雨交加的夜路。

266

我不請你進入我的屋裏；
我的愛人啊，
請你進入我無限的寂寞吧。

267

死，一如生，
屬於生命的一部分。
行走一步，起於舉足，
一如止於落足。

268

您同花和陽光的喁喁細語，
我已能明白，
它們的意義很單純。
告訴我吧，讓我也明白，
您在痛苦和死亡中
所傾吐的是怎樣的話語。

CCLXIX

The night's flower was late when the morning kissed her, she shivered and sighed and dropped to the ground.

CCLXX

Through the sadness of all things I hear the crooning of the Eternal Mother.

CCLXXI

I came to your shore as a stranger, I lived in your house as a guest, I leave your door as a friend, my earth.

CCLXXII

Let my thoughts come to you, when I am gone, like the afterglow of sunset at the margin of starry silence.

269

夜之花開得很遲，
經晨光一吻，便化為
一陣戰慄，一聲嘆息，
而凋落地上。

270

我從萬物的悲戚中，
聽見永恆之母的呻吟。

271

我登上你的岸，是一位陌生人，
我住進你的屋，是一位客人，
而今，我的大地啊，
我告別你的門，成了你的朋友。

272

我去後，
讓我的思念來伴著你，
像倚偎在靜穆的星空邊緣，
那一抹落日餘暉。

CCLXXIII

Light in my heart the evening star of rest and then let the night whisper to me of love.

CCLXXIV

I am a child in the dark.
I stretch my hands through the coverlet of night for thee, Mother.

CCLXXV

The day of work is done. Hide my face in your arms, Mother.
Let me dream.

CCLXXVI

The lamp of meeting burns long; it goes out in a moment at the parting.

273

請在我的心中點亮
那代表安息的黃昏之星，
讓夜向我耳邊傾吐愛的絮語。

274

我是一個
迷失在黑暗中的孩子。
我伸出雙手，刺破覆蓋著萬物的夜幕，
來擁抱您呀，母親。

275

做完一天的工作。
母親啊，
把我的頭埋在你的懷裏吧，
讓我做個好夢。

276

相聚之燈，不覺長明；
離別之時，滅於一瞬。

CCLXXVII

One word keep for me in thy silence,
O World, when I am dead,
"I have loved."

CCLXXVIII

We live in this world when we love it.

CCLXXIX

Let the dead have the immortality of fame, but the living the immortality of love.

CCLXXX

I have seen thee as the half-awakened child sees his mother in the dusk of the dawn and then smiles and sleeps again.

277

大世界啊，我死後
請在您的緘默中，
為我保留一句話——
我曾經愛過。

278

吾人生於此世，
惟賴人人有愛。

279

讓死去的享不朽之名；
讓活著的享不朽之愛。

280

我曾經見過您——
當時我的感覺，
就像一個半睡半醒的嬰孩，
在黎明的微光中，
看見他的母親，
然後，笑一笑又睡著了。

CCLXXXI

I shall die again and again to know that
life is inexhaustible.

CCLXXXII

While I was passing with the crowd in the
road I saw thy smile from the balcony
and I sang and forgot all noise.

CCLXXXIII

Love is life in its fulness like the cup
with its wine.

CCLXXXIV

They light their own lamps and sing their
own words in their temples.
But the birds sing thy name in thine own
morning light, for thy name is joy.

281

我將一次又一次地死去，
藉以認識生命的無限。

282

我跟著一群行人路過，
瞥見您從陽台上投來的微笑，
我不禁縱聲高歌，
忘卻一切周遭的塵囂。

283

生命裏注滿了愛，
猶如酒杯斟滿了酒。

284

他們燃他們的燈，
唱他們的歌曲，
拜他們的神廟。
但鳥兒歌著您的名字，
沐著您的晨光——
您的名字就叫做歡樂。

CCLXXXV

Lead me in the centre of thy silence to
fill my heart with songs.

CCLXXXVI

Let them live who choose in their own
hissing world of fireworks.
My heart longs for thy stars, my God.

CCLXXXVII

Love's pain sang round my life like the
unplumbed sea, and love's joy sang
like birds in its flowering groves.

CCLXXXVIII

Put out the lamp when thou wishest.
I shall know thy darkness and
shall love it.

285

引導我進入您的沉默之殿，
給我的心靈注滿歌曲。

286

讓他們甘願囿居於
煙火嗤嗤的塵世中吧。
我的上帝啊，
我的心靈渴望您的星光。

287

愛的悲吟，
困圍著我的生命，
有如深不可測的大海；
愛的喜悅，
彷彿小鳥在花林中的歡唱。

288

如果您願意，
就請熄滅您的燈吧。
我會明白黑暗底意義，
我會喜歡它。

CCLXXXIX

When I stand before thee at the day's end thou shalt see my scars and know that I had my wounds and also my healing.

CCXC

Some day I shall sing to thee in the sunrise of some other world, "I have seen thee before in the light of the earth, in the love of man."

CCXCI

Clouds come floating into my life from other days no longer to shed rain or usher storm but to give colour to my sunset sky.

CCXCII

Truth raises against itself the storm that scatters its seeds broadcast.

289

白日已盡，
當我站在您的面前，
您仍能看見我的疤痕，
了解我受過創傷，
但已痊癒。

290

將來有一天，
我會從另一世界的日出，
對您歌唱——
我以前曾見過您，
在大地之光中，
在人類的愛裏。

291

往日的浮雲，
飄入我的生命，
已不再帶來狂風暴雨，
只給我的夕空
塗上彩霞。

292

真理激起反面的風暴，
藉以散播它的種子。

CCXCIII

The storm of last night has crowned this morning with golden peace.

CCXCIV

Truth seems to come with its final word; and the final word gives birth to its next.

CCXCV

Blessed is he whose fame does not outshine his truth.

CCXCVI

Sweetness of thy name fills my heart when I forget mine—like thy morning sun when the mist is melted.

293

昨夜的暴風雨，
給今朝的寧靜冠上金冕。

294

真理似乎總跟著一條定律；
而此定律復衍生次一定律。

295

名聲不掩過「真相」的人，
上帝會賜福他。

296

每當我忘了自己的名字，
您的甜蜜的名字
便照亮我的心靈，
有如雲散霧盡的朝陽。

CCXCVII

The silent night has the beauty of the mother and the clamorous day of the child.

CCXCVIII

The world loved man when he smiled.
The world became afraid of him when he laughed.

CCXCIX

God waits for man to regain his childhood in wisdom.

CCC

Let me feel this world as thy love taking form, then my love will help it.

297

寧靜的夜晚有母親的美，
喧嚷的白日有孩子的美。

298

人微笑時世界愛他；
大笑時世界變得怕他。

299

上帝期待世人
應用智慧拾回童年。

300

讓我想像這世界
乃是您的愛的化身，
我也將用愛來相助。

CCCI

Thy sunshine smiles upon the winter days of my heart, never doubting of its spring flowers.

CCCII

God kisses the finite in his love and man the infinite.

CCCIII

Thou crossest desert lands of barren years to reach the moment of fulfilment.

CCCIV

God's silence ripens man's thoughts into speech.

301

您的和煦的陽光，
照耀在我心靈的冬天，
從不置疑其未來的春花。

302

上帝愛世人之有限，
世人愛上帝之無限。

303

您渡過多少荒年與荒漠，
以追求瞬間的成就。

304

上帝的緘默，
將人的思想培育成語言。

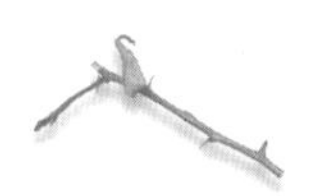

CCCV

Thou wilt find, Eternal Traveller, marks of thy footsteps across my songs.

CCCVI

Let me not shame thee, Father, who displayest thy glory in thy children.

CCCVII

Cheerless is the day, the light under frowning clouds is like a punished child with traces of tears on its pale cheeks, and the cry of the wind is like the cry of a wounded world. But I know I am travelling to meet my Friend.

CCCVIII

To-night there is a stir among the palm leaves, a swell in the sea, Full Moon, like the heart-throb of the world. From what unknown sky hast thou carried in thy silence the aching secret of love?

305

永恆的旅人啊，
您將在我的詩歌裏，
隨處發現您的足跡。

306

父親啊，
您把光輝展示在孩子身上；
讓我不會使您蒙羞。

307

那是一個沒有歡笑的日子——
烏雲縫隙漏下的絲絲陽光，
像一個受罰的小孩
掛在蒼頰上一行行的淚痕。
風的呻吟象徵受創的世界，
然而我知道我不辭跋涉，
只為了去會我的「神友」。

308

今天夜晚，
棕櫚樹葉間忽生一陣騷動，
海上也湧起一股浪潮，
像世界的心在狂跳。
滿滿的月兒啊，
您打什麼不可知的天宮，
悄悄捎來痛苦的愛底秘密？

CCCIX

I dream of a star, an island of light, where I shall be born and in the depth of its quickening leisure my life will ripen its works like the rice-field in the autumn sun.

CCCX

The smell of the wet earth in the rain rises like a great chant of praise from the voiceless multitude of the insignificant.

CCCXI

That love can ever lose is a fact that we cannot accept as truth.

CCCXII

We shall know some day that death can never rob us of that which our soul has gained, for her gains are one with herself.

309

我夢想天邊有一顆星——
那是一個光明之島，
我將在那兒誕生，
趁那兒絲毫無塵務之擾，
加速成長，成熟，
完成我的人生使命，
彷彿那秋陽下的稻田。

310

雨中濡溼的泥土，
散發出一片馥郁之氣，
有如來自沉默的平民大眾之，
一場無聲的讚美詩大合唱。

311

愛，難免有時會失敗，
這雖是一個事實，
但不能視為真理。

312

我們有一天會明白，
死亡永不可能奪走
我們靈魂的所有，
因為靈魂的所有，
與其本身是一體的。

CCCXIII

God comes to me in the dusk of my evening
with the flowers from my past kept
fresh in his basket.

CCCXIV

When all the strings of my life will be
tuned, my Master, then at every touch
of thine will come out the music
of love.

CCCXV

Let me live truly, my Lord, so that
death to me become true.

CCCXVI

Man's history is waiting in patience
for the triumph of the insulted man.

313

上帝在我的暮色蒼茫中，
給我帶來我的昔日之花，
而花在他的花籃中，
還保存得很新鮮。

314

我把生命的琴弦
所有的弦音都調好時，
我的主啊，
您每觸動一下，
奏出的都是愛的音樂。

315

我的主啊，
讓我活得真實，
俾我也死得真實。

316

人類的歷史
就是耐心的等待，
等待那被侮辱者的勝利。

CCCXVII

I feel thy gaze upon my heart this moment like the sunny silence of the morning upon the lonely field whose harvest is over.

CCCXVIII

I long for the Island of Songs across this heaving Sea of Shouts.

CCCXIX

The prelude of the night is commenced in the music of the sunset, in its solemn hymn to the ineffable dark.

CCCXX

I have scaled the peak and found no shelter in fame's bleak and barren height. Lead me, my Guide, before the light fades, into the valley of quiet where life's harvest mellows into golden wisdom.

317

此刻我感覺到，
您正凝視著我的心，
一如默默的朝陽，
照耀著秋收後的落寞田野。

318

我渴望渡過這
波濤洶湧的「咆哮之海」，
到那彼岸的「詩歌之島」。

319

夜的序曲開始了——
落日的音樂
奏起莊嚴的聖歌，
頌讚著神奇無比的黑暗。

320

浮生虛名，
如一片荒寒的高原，
我攀爬過它的峰頂，
卻不可得一棲身之所。
我的嚮導啊，
在日色漸沒之前，
領我到那靜穆的山谷，
人生的收穫在那兒
醞釀成熟而結出金的智慧。

CCCXXI

Things look phantastic in this dimness of the dusk—the spires whose bases are lost in the dark and tree-tops like blots of ink. I shall wait for the morning and wake up to see thy city in the light.

CCCXXII

I have suffered and despaired and known death and I am glad that I am in this great world.

CCCXXIII

There are tracts in my life that are bare and silent. They are the open spaces where my busy days had their light and air.

321

在這朦朧的暮靄裏，
一切都顯得十分詭異——
尖塔的基座被黑暗吞噬了，
樹梢好似斑斑墨漬。
我將等待清晨醒來，
在光明中再見您的城。

322

我曾受難過，
絕望過，
認識過死亡；
現在我很高興，
能活在這個大世界中。

323

在我的生命裏，
有一些荒涼不毛之地。
我的忙碌日子，
就在這片空間，
吸取陽光和空氣。

CCCXXIV

Release me from my unfulfilled past clinging to me from behind making death difficult.

CCCXXV

Let this be my last word, that I trust in thy love.

324

救救我吧——
多少過去的遺恨，
從背後緊攀著我，
使我求死也難。

325

讓我獻此最後的心語：
我信賴您的愛。

——一九九六年七月二十三日完稿

Stray Birds

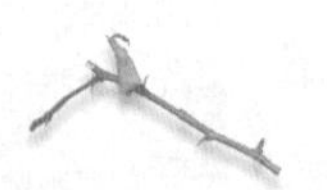

譯者以七言絕句衍譯撼人心弦的《魯拜集》，天才橫溢，文采斐然，媲美英譯。奧瑪珈音有「波斯李白」之稱，在縱酒狂歌的表象之下，洞澈生命的虛幻無常。

「黃先生譯詩雅貼比美 Fitzgerald 原譯。Fitzgerald 書札中論譯事屢云『寧爲活麻雀，不做死鷹』，(better a live sparrow than a dead eagle)，況活鷹乎？」

錢鍾書(文學家）

楊德豫所譯拜倫詩歌在大陸有多種版本，總印數達五十萬冊以上，被著名老詩人、翻譯家卞之琳譽爲「標誌著我國譯詩藝術的成熟」。這本《拜倫抒情詩選》共六十二首（段），二千二百餘行。不但包括了拜倫抒情短詩中的所有精品，還從拜倫的多種長詩和詩劇中選譯了若干精彩的插曲或片段。從長詩《唐璜》中節譯的〈海蒂之死〉長達三百六十行。譯者堅持「以格律詩譯格律詩」，原詩的格律以及譯詩所採用的相應的格律，都在每首譯詩的題註中作了具體說明。本書還附錄了譯者的重要論文〈用什麼形式翻譯英語格律詩〉。

本書精選詩作近一百七十首，選譯自代表詩集如：《葦叢中的風》(The Wind Among the Reeds)、《在那七片樹林裡》(In the Seven Woods)、《庫勒的野天鵝》(The Wild Swans at Coole)、《塔堡》(The Tower)、《旋梯及其他》(The Winding Stair and Other Poems)等。譯文忠實原詩意蘊，摹擬原詩形式及韻律。譯者傅浩，長年研究葉慈其人其詩，爲序簡述葉慈生平，包括對愛爾蘭的民族情感、在政治運動中所持立場、個人起伏複雜的感情生活、對神祕主義的愛好、對詩藝的追求與演變等，提供了解葉慈詩作精要之背景。書末附葉慈年表及詩作索引。

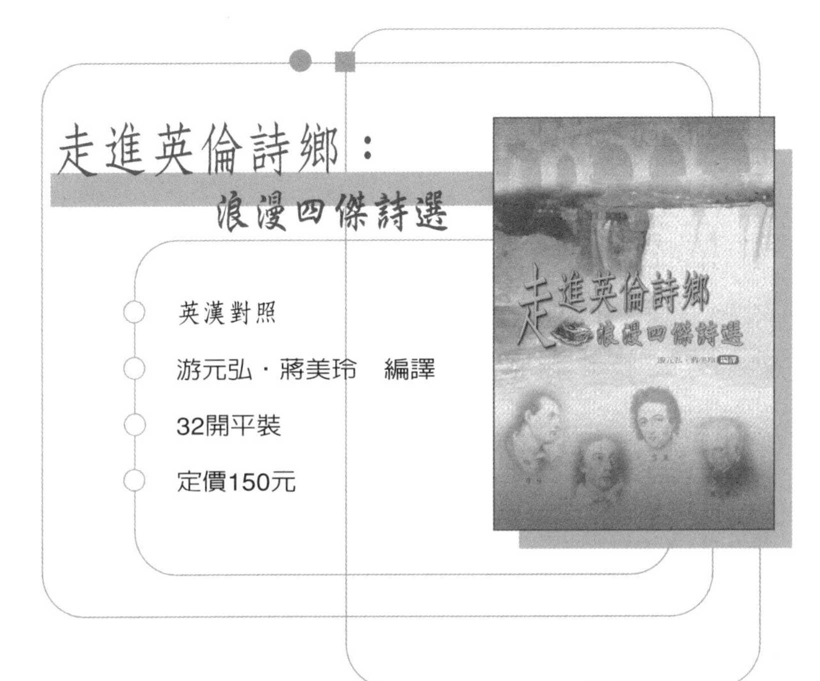

浪漫時期英詩以平實的語言，抒發個人生命經驗湧現的感動，開啓詩的新紀元：華茲華斯的山水詩富於哲思「大自然從未叛離愛它的人心」、「大自然活化你我的內心，以靜和美」；濟慈「美即是眞，眞即是美」、「燦亮之星，願我像你一樣堅定」；雪萊「風啊，冬天到來，春天還會遠嗎？」；拜倫「她行於美中，恰似夜晚無雲的天空滿佈星斗」。本書選譯最能代表浪漫時期特性的詩作，譯筆簡淨流暢，富於詩的節奏與韻味，這些名詩能使人在心境困頓時得到安慰，更能淨化性靈，美化愛情的心，是人生中不容錯過的好詩，值得您細細品讀。

書林詩叢／詩集／譯詩／詩論

〔詩集 1〕錄影詩學　羅青著……………………100
〔詩集 2〕如果愛情像口香糖　王添源著……………………100
〔詩集 3〕都市終端機　林燿德著……………………140
〔詩集 4〕紙上風雲　簡政珍著……………………100
〔詩集 5〕夢或者黎明及其他　商禽著……………………150
〔詩集 6〕這首詩可能還不錯　嚴力著……………………120
〔詩集 8〕苦苓的政治詩　苦苓著……………………120
〔詩集 9〕親密書：陳黎詩選 (1974～1992)　陳黎著……………………150
★1993 年國家文藝獎詩歌類獎章★　★1992 年聯合報文學類最佳書獎★　★2000 年吳三連文學獎★
〔詩集 10〕S.L.和寶藍色筆記　孟樊著……………………120
〔詩集 11〕獻給雨季的歌　譚石著……………………100
〔詩集 12〕沒有一朵雲需要國界　白靈著……………………150
〔詩集 13〕雪崩——洛夫詩選　洛夫著……………………150
〔詩集 14〕夢的圖解　洛夫著……………………150
〔詩集 15〕飄泊者　張錯著……………………150
〔詩集 16〕蟬的發芽　羅葉著……………………150
〔詩集 17〕薔薇花事　斯人著……………………150
〔詩集 18〕從聽診器的那端　江自得著……………………120
〔詩集 19〕春夜無聲　張錯著……………………120
〔詩集 20〕我的近代史——台灣詩錄　張信吉著……………………150
〔詩集 21〕美麗深邃的亞細亞　陳克華著……………………150
★2001 年台北市文學獎★
〔詩集 22〕異形 ★2001 年台北市文學獎★　孫維民著……………………120
〔詩集 23〕冥想乃現實　簫蘇著……………………120
〔詩集 24〕陳黎詩集 I：1973-1993　陳黎著……………………300
★2000 年吳三連文學獎★
〔詩集 25〕新世代詩人精選集　簡政珍主編……………………350
〔詩集 26〕在芝加哥的微光中　奎澤石頭著……………………180
〔詩集 27〕城市的靈魂　陳家帶著……………………150
〔詩集 28〕滾動原鄉　鍾喬著……………………120
〔詩集 29〕沒有非結不可的果　非馬著……………………180
〔詩集 30〕夢蜻蜓　謝昭華著……………………150
〔詩集 31〕花與淚與河流　陳克華著……………………150
〔詩集 32〕滄桑男子　張錯著……………………150

Stray Birds

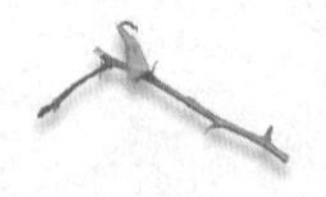

Stray Birds

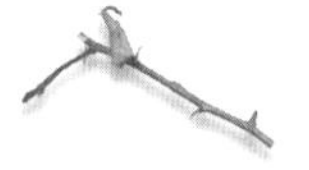

Stray Birds

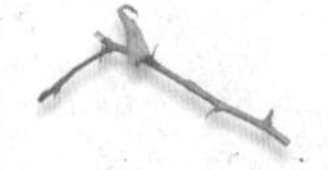